OTHER YEARLING BOOKS YOU WILL ENJOY:

LOVE ME, LOVE MY WEREWOLF, *Stephen Roos*
MY HORRIBLE SECRET, *Stephen Roos*
MY SECRET ADMIRER, *Stephen Roos*
THE TERRIBLE TRUTH, *Stephen Roos*
TWELVE-YEAR-OLD VOWS REVENGE!, *Stephen Roos*
HOW TO EAT FRIED WORMS, *Thomas Rockwell*
HOW TO FIGHT A GIRL, *Thomas Rockwell*
HOW TO GET FABULOUSLY RICH, *Thomas Rockwell*
BOBBY BASEBALL, *Robert Kimmel Smith*
CHOCOLATE FEVER, *Robert Kimmel Smith*

YEARLING BOOKS/YOUNG YEARLINGS/YEARLING CLASSICS are designed especially to entertain and enlighten young people. Patricia Reilly Giff, consultant to this series, received her bachelor's degree from Marymount College and a master's degree in history from St. John's University. She holds a Professional Diploma in Reading and a Doctorate of Humane Letters from Hofstra University. She was a teacher and reading consultant for many years, and is the author of numerous books for young readers.

For a complete listing of all Yearling titles,
write to Dell Readers Service,
P.O. Box 1045, South Holland, IL 60473.

● THE PET LOVERS CLUB ●

Crocodile Christmas

STEPHEN ROOS

Illustrated by **Jacqueline Rogers**

A Yearling Book

Published by
Dell Publishing
a division of
Bantam Doubleday Dell Publishing Group, Inc.
1540 Broadway
New York, New York 10036

ISBN 0-440-40872-5

Reprinted by arrangement with Delacorte Press

Printed in the United States of America

October 1993

10 9 8 7 6 5 4 3 2 1

CWO

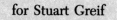
for Stuart Greif

Contents

Crocodile Christmas

Chapter 1

C_-R-E-A-K!_

Slowly Lem pushed the heavy wooden door shut.

He blinked.

Then he blinked again.

After the glare of the sun on the snow outdoors, Lem had to blink half a dozen times before he could focus.

The Mossmans' basement was the only one on Pulaski Street that hadn't been turned into a rec room or a workshop. The floor was cement, the walls were cinder block, and the only light came from the 60-watt bulb that dangled from the middle of the ceiling.

One side was mostly Mr. Mossman's tools, all hanging on hooks, the lawn mower, the hedge clipper, two sprinklers, and three rakes.

The other side was mostly the hot water heater and the furnace.

The rest was mostly old summer furniture arranged in a circle under the naked light bulb.

Sitting in all but two of the chairs were most of the Pet Lovers Club.

"Lem! You're late!" called a girl wearing thick glasses with big blue frames.

"Sorry," Lem muttered.

Quickly he took off his winter coat, his scarf, and his red woolen mittens. He took off the red woolen cap that covered his sand-colored hair, kicked off his boots, and plopped himself down next to Wylie.

Bang!

Bang!

Bang!

The girl with the glasses pounded the side of the furnace with the flat of her hand. "The Pet Lovers Club will now come to order!" she announced in a loud, clear voice.

The girl's name was Erin. On her lap was a big floppy black-and-white rabbit.

The rabbit's name was Peter and he was munching on a carrot Erin was holding out for him.

Lem looked around at the other Pet Lovers.

Bernie sat next to Erin.

He was patting his dog's neck.

Bernie and Erin had started Pet Lovers at the beginning of the third grade. There was a meeting once every week in Erin's basement, and almost every month Dr. Miller, the retired vet who lived on the block, took the kids on a field trip. Any third-grader at Turkey Hill Elementary was welcome to join, but what with Cub Scouts, Brownies, piano lessons, and dentist appointments, not everyone who was a member could show up at every meeting.

Tammy was sitting on the other side of Bernie.

She was stroking her Siamese cat's back.

Norris was tapping the side of his goldfish bowl.

Becka was rubbing the Lucite box with her two pet cockroaches inside.

Sitting on Lem's right was Wylie. Wylie was scratching his hamster behind the ears.

Lem didn't have a pet.

Neither did Dirty Donald, who was sitting on Lem's left.

Lem looked at Dirty Donald, who was wiping dried green glop from the side of his face. It was the split pea soup from lunch at Turkey Hill Elementary. Donald was always wearing his last meal.

It was no wonder the kids called him Dirty Donald!

"Don't forget to feed your pet," Erin sang to the tune of "Row, Row, Row Your Boat." It was the beginning of the Pet Lovers Club anthem, and the kids sang it at each meeting.

"And check its water too!" all the other Pet Lovers chimed in.

C–R–E–A–K!

As soon as he felt the blast of ice-cold air, Lem stopped singing.

So did the rest of the Pet Lovers.

Marsha was standing in the doorway. In both of her hands were shopping bags.

"Marsha!" Erin exclaimed impatiently.

"I know I'm late," Marsha said with a sigh, "but I couldn't help it."

As Marsha took off her down parka with the hood, Lem noticed the braids that went all the way down to her waist. They were so long that Lem figured she had started growing them as soon as she had been born.

"What did you forget this time?" Tammy asked.

"Marsha always forgets *something*," Dirty Donald whispered to Lem.

Even though Lem already knew how forgetful Marsha was, he nodded happily. Lem had moved into the neighborhood only two months before, and the Pet Lovers were still going out of their way to make him feel comfortable. So far joining Pet Lovers was the best thing about moving, Lem thought.

"This time I remembered *everything*," Marsha bragged.

"Even the cookies?" Dirty Donald asked suspiciously.

Marsha held out one shopping bag for him to take.

"Did you remember the Christmas wreath?" Tammy asked.

Marsha held out the other shopping bag for Tammy.

Then she sat down next to Erin.

Marsha was the third member of Pet Lovers who didn't have a pet yet.

Bang!
Bang!
Bang!

"*Now* can we bring the meeting of the Pet Lovers to order?" Erin asked as she slapped the furnace again.

Donald was ripping open the box of cookies.

"Christmas tree cookies?" he asked sadly. "Yuck!"

"But it's almost Christmas," Marsha reminded him.

"But I love marshmallow cookies," Dirty Donald moaned.

"The wreath's pretty," Tammy said as she attached it to a hook that hung beside the furnace.

"It's pretty," Dirty Donald admitted, "but you can't eat it."

He stuffed three cookie Christmas trees into his mouth. They were green.

Lem watched the crumbs fall all over his chin.

"Maybe we should just skip the anthem," Erin groaned.

"No! No! No!" shouted the Pet Lovers.

"Okay," Erin said, "but if we don't make it all

the way through, let's table the anthem till the next meeting."

"*Now!*" all the Pet Lovers shouted back at her.

"Don't forget to feed your pet," Erin sang out.

"And check its water too!" all the Pet Lovers sang now.

"When it's sick, go see the vet.
Your pet depends on you!

"Clean its home out once a week,
Its hutch or cage or bowl.
Tend its broken tail or beak.
Pet Loving is our goal!

"Pet Lovers are a noble breed.
We're loyal, brave, and true!
If you agree, come on and be
A Pet Lover too!"

"Hooray! Hooray! Hooray!" the Pet Lovers shouted.

The kids clapped as hard as they could.

"What's the first order of business?" Erin asked.

"The trip to the zoo!" Bernie exclaimed. His hair was almost white and cut so short that sometimes it looked as if he didn't have any hair at all.

"The zoo! The zoo! The zoo!" the Pet Lovers shouted.

Lem shouted along with the others. He had been excited about the trip from the first.

"The hot dogs there are the best!" Dirty Donald exclaimed, stuffing two more Christmas trees into his mouth. "So everyone remember their lunch money."

"But admission is free for kids," Erin reminded everyone.

"Good thing too," Bernie said. "That way I'll have enough money left over for Elton's Christmas present."

He gave his dog's scruffy head an extra scratch.

"What are you getting him?" Norris asked.

Bernie put his hands over Elton's ears. "A special collar," he whispered. "I've had my eye on it for weeks."

"Are you getting a Christmas present for your goldfish?" Erin asked Norris.

"My family celebrates Hanukkah," Norris said, "so I'm getting my goldfish a Hanukkah present. Maybe a new filter or some designer rocks."

"I haven't figured out what to give Mercedes this year," Wylie admitted. "Last year she wanted comic books and candy bars."

"That's nuts!" Erin said. "Hamsters don't eat candy and they can't read either!"

"Mercedes likes to see me eat candy and read comic books. It's *her* idea of a good time."

Everyone laughed, the way they usually did at the things Wylie said.

"I'm getting a Christmas present for my parrot!" Marsha said excitedly.

"Ahhhh!" the Pet Lovers sighed as they sat up in their seats.

"You're getting a parrot?" Wylie asked.

"It's coming any day now!" Marsha squealed. "All the way from South America! It's costing a bundle too. Almost a thousand dollars!"

"A thousand dollars?" Tammy asked, shaking her head so hard that all her red curls jiggled.

"For a pet?" Bernie asked.

"Does it talk?" Erin asked.

"For a thousand bucks, it *better* talk plenty!" Becka said.

"Parrots are very rare," Marsha explained. "And they're hard to catch too. They only come from the jungle! That's why they cost so much."

"What's it matter what a pet costs?" Wylie asked. "Mercedes was a dollar fifty and she's perfect."

"Peter cost only five dollars," Erin said as she scratched him behind the ears.

"Elton was free," Bernie boasted.

"So were the cockroaches," Becka said as she snapped the suspenders she always wore over her T-shirt. "I caught them in the wild. It was a very beautiful experience."

"*What* wild?" Marsha asked suspiciously.

"Under the kitchen sink," Becka said.

"That's not the wild," Marsha said.

"Try telling that to a cockroach," Becka said.

"What are you getting the roaches for Christmas?" Wylie giggled.

"Hard to say," Becka admitted. "They like almost everything."

Lem turned to Dirty Donald. "You're not getting a pet too, are you?" he asked.

"Oh, didn't I tell you?" Dirty Donald asked. "I'm getting a guinea pig for Christmas!"

"Now there will be two pigs in your house," Wylie laughed.

When Dirty Donald laughed along with Wylie, everyone else laughed too.

Except Lem.

He was thinking.

He felt a hand on his shoulder. It was Wylie's.

"What's the matter?" Wylie whispered. "Why are you looking so sad?"

"I guess I feel bad about not having a pet," Lem admitted.

"It's not like you have to have one to be in Pet Lovers," Becka said.

"All you have to do is love pets and want to talk about them," Erin added.

"You have to want to help them too!" Bernie said.

"And you have to go to third grade," Dirty Donald reminded everyone. "It's in the bylaws."

"Well, Lem does all that, so there's no problem," Marsha pointed out.

"Yeah," Lem sighed. "But when you and Donald get your pets, I'm going to be the *only* Pet Lover without a pet."

"Does your mom think you're too young to have a pet?" Becka asked.

"Oh, no," Lem said, shifting uncomfortably about in his seat. "She didn't say I was too young."

"Does she think you can't handle the responsibility yet?" Erin asked.

"I can take care of a pet," Lem said. "My mom knows that!"

"Then why won't she let you have one?" Norris asked.

"I don't know just what pet I want is all," Lem said. "But as soon as I decide, my mom'll get it for me."

"Gee," Becka said. "I thought you might have a *real* problem."

"That's a *nice* problem," Erin said.

"There are so many neat pets to choose from," Bernie said.

"Yeah, I can have a pet any old time," Lem said with as big a smile as he could get his lips to make. "I don't have anything to worry about."

He looked from face to face.

All the kids were nodding happily.

Except Wylie. Wylie was shaking his head, just a little.

"It's the truth, Wylie," Lem said. "Honest."

But Wylie still didn't smile.

Lem bit his lip, the way he did when he was

nervous about something. Even if Wylie did know it wasn't the *whole* truth, Lem wasn't going to say one more word about it.

Some things were too hard to talk about, even to the Pet Lovers.

Chapter 2

A blast of icy wind whooshed up Pulaski Street.

Lem pulled his red cap down tighter over his head. The wind was so cold that a tear fell over his freckles. Lem wiped it away with his mitten.

"Hey, Lem!"

Lem walked on.

The week before it had snowed. The sidewalks were icy and Lem had to be careful not to slip.

"Hey, Lem. Wait up!"

Lem was concentrating so hard on the ice that he didn't hear Wylie.

Whiz!

A snowball flew just above Lem's head!

Splat!

Lem jumped back just as the snowball hit the side of the mailbox.

Plop!

The snowball fell to the sidewalk.

"Hey, what's the big idea?" he shouted, turning on his heels.

The first thing Lem saw were Wylie's eyebrows. They were thick and black and they met just above his nose.

"Didn't you hear me?" Wylie asked.

Lem shrugged.

Wylie ran to catch up with him.

Soon the two boys were walking together down Pulaski Street.

"You're worried about the pet stuff, aren't you?" Wylie asked.

"I am not!" Lem declared. "Didn't you hear me at the meeting?"

"But I know it's not just because you can't decide what kind of pet you want," Wylie said quietly. "It's something else too, isn't it?"

Suddenly Lem felt his face getting red. "It's private," he said anxiously.

Wylie stopped in his tracks. "I didn't mean to butt in," he said. "You want to be by yourself?"

"Yeah," Lem said. "Sorry."

The boys kept walking side by side.

"You going to play with the other kids now?" Lem asked.

"I'll stick with you," Wylie said.

"How can I be by myself if you're here?"

"Well, if you can't be by yourself with a friend, who *can* you be all by yourself with?" Wylie asked.

Lem couldn't help smiling.

Even though Lem and his mom and his little brother Stuart had moved in next to Wylie's family only recently, Lem felt as if he'd been Wylie's friend for a long, long time.

The boys walked past Norris's house with the menorah in the window.

Past Dr. Miller's house with the little manger on the lawn.

Dr. Miller was the retired vet who was taking the Pet Lovers to the zoo.

When the boys got to Marsha's house, they stopped.

The front door had the biggest Christmas wreath in town on it.

The windows had the biggest Christmas candles.

But it was the roof that Lem couldn't keep his eye off of. Most of the other houses on Pulaski Street had slanting roofs. The roof on Marsha's house was flat.

There, on the roof, were all of Santa's reindeer! Behind the reindeer was Santa's sleigh, and in the sleigh was a life-size Santa Claus.

Every night, when all the lights were on, cars drove up and down Pulaski Street just to see Santa Claus and all the reindeer on Marsha's roof.

"Marsha's mom and dad hired six men to put all that stuff up there." Lem said. "Her family really *is* rich."

"Who cares?" Wylie said. "You want to go over to the Hot Shoppe with me?"

Lem took off his mitten.

He stuck his hand into his pocket.

Two quarters and some pennies.

Not enough.

"Nah," he said. "It's too crowded at the Hot Shoppe and the older kids are always pushing."

The boys turned the corner onto Blueberry Lane.

"What else could we do?" asked Lem.

"We could go to my house," Wylie said.

"Would your mom make us tuna sandwiches?" Lem asked.

"I thought we didn't like tuna anymore," Wylie said.

"Since when?" Lem asked.

"Since you got sick on the tuna noodle casserole at school," Wylie said, "and we promised we'd never eat it again."

"It was the *noodles* that got me sick," Lem said. "That's what we promised to be allergic to."

"Gee, I'm glad you told me," Wylie said. "I could have been getting sick on tuna when all along I should have been getting sick on noodles."

Lem laughed.

"If you come over, we could play with Mercedes," Wylie said.

Wylie unzipped the top of his coat.

Mercedes poked her head from the pocket on the front of Wylie's shirt.

"Mercedes is neat," Lem said, stroking the warm fur on her back with his finger.

"You'll have a pet of your own someday," Wylie said.

Suddenly Lem was feeling uncomfortable all over again. "I guess I won't come over to your

house after all," he said. "I got to go home now, Wylie."

"You sure?"

"My mom needs me," Lem said. "I forgot about it."

Wylie waved his right mitten in the air.

Lem watched him walk up to his own house.

It wasn't so big as Marsha's but it was nice.

Through the picture window, Lem could see an enormous Christmas tree with more bulbs and lights than Lem thought you could fit on a tree.

There were candles in the windows and a wreath on the door too.

It looked like a Christmas card, Lem thought.

Lem walked on.

His house was at the end of the street, just beyond the foundation that no one wanted to build anything on.

It was small.

It needed a paint job too.

It wasn't anything like the house with the above-ground pool and the two-car garage that his family had lived in before his dad died.

Lem stuck his hand back into his pocket.

He started to count up the change again.

Even though he knew it was still going to be the same two quarters and the pennies that had been there before, he just couldn't help hoping that this time it would be more.

Chapter 3

Lem closed the door behind him and looked around the kitchen.

It was smaller than the old kitchen.

The refrigerator was old.

But as his mom said, it worked.

The stove was old, but it worked too.

Stuart was sitting at the kitchen table. His hair was neatly combed, and there weren't any smudges on his face or his clothes either. Stuart was four and a half, and everyone said he was a Perfect Little Angel. As far as Lem was concerned, Perfect Little Angels could be Royal Pains sometimes.

On the table were neat little piles of colored

paper. Two bottles of glue and a pair of small red scissors were neatly arranged on a newspaper.

"Ma!" Lem yelled out loud as he kicked off his boots. "I'm home!"

Stuart looked up.

"Your boots go on the newspaper," Stuart reminded him, pointing to a newspaper on the floor beside the stove.

Lem picked up his boots and put them there.

"Where's Ma?" Lem asked.

"Upstairs, talking to Grandpa."

Stuart was trying to snip the red paper into strips. So far Stuart wasn't having much luck. Each strip was looking more like scrap paper.

"Grandpa's here?" Lem asked as he unzipped his coat and let it fall onto the linoleum. "His truck isn't out front."

"Coat goes on the hook," Stuart said.

"Where's Grandpa?" Lem asked.

"On the phone," Stuart said, tearing the paper now.

Pop!

Ping!

Pop!

"What's that?" Lem asked.

Stuart pointed to the pot on the stove.

"Popcorn," Stuart said.

"Oh, good," Lem said, rubbing the palms of his hands happily. "I'm starving."

"It's for the tree," Stuart said.

"Huh?" Lem asked. "What's a tree need popcorn for?"

"It goes with the cranberries," Stuart said, ripping pieces of yellow paper into strips. "I bet you don't know what I'm doing, Lem."

"Making another nuclear reactor?" Lem asked as he opened the refrigerator.

"I'm making paper chains," Stuart said. "It goes yellow, then red, then blue, then orange, then pink, then black."

"Mom isn't saving that piece of chocolate cake for anything, is she?" Lem asked as he took the plate out of the refrigerator. He reached into a drawer for a fork. Then he put the plate on the table and sat down.

"Mom didn't say you could eat that," Stuart said.

"Mom doesn't want me to starve to death," Lem said.

"Mom doesn't want you to spoil your appetite either."

Lem looked up, a forkful of chocolate cake still in his mouth.

His mom was standing in the doorway.

She was wearing jeans and a flannel shirt and she was dragging the vacuum cleaner behind her. She was pretty even when she was cleaning. That was more than Lem could say about some of the other moms he had seen.

Lem took the fork from his mouth.

Most of the cake was still on it.

"I'm really starving, Mom," Lem explained, waving the fork in the air.

"Didn't they have cookies at Pet Lovers?" Stuart asked.

"Donald ate them all," Lem said.

"Enjoy the cake, honey," his mom said.

She pushed the vacuum into the corner and mussed up Lem's hair.

Usually he hated it when she did that.

Today he didn't mind because it meant he was off the hook.

"Grandpa's coming," she said. "Day after to-morrow."

"For Christmas?" Lem asked.

"Maybe longer," their mom said. "Someone bought his farm. It's all settled."

She took the popcorn off the stove and poured it into a bowl.

Lem sat up in his chair. "Does that mean Grandpa's rich now?" he asked hopefully.

"It means he's okay if he's careful," his mother said. "The way we'll be just as soon as I get a regular job."

Lem's mom did office work two or three days a week but it didn't pay enough. What she needed was a full-time job that paid better and had health insurance and day care so she wouldn't have to leave Stuart with the neighbors when she was working.

"Pet Lovers are going to the zoo," Lem reminded his mom.

His mother took her bag from the hook beside the door. "You need the lunch money, right?"

Lem kept looking at his lap. He hated asking for money these days. "I could take a bag lunch," he said cautiously. "I don't *have* to buy lunch there."

"The other kids are buying theirs, aren't they?" his mom asked.

Lem nodded.

His mom took out her change purse and gave Lem three dollars.

Lem stuffed them into his pocket.

"I'd rather go to the pet shop, Mom," Lem said. He'd promised he wouldn't ask again, but the words were out of his mouth before he could stop them.

"Lem, I already told you," his mother said.

"I'm sorry, Ma . . ." Lem said sadly.

"Is Santa at the pet shop?" Stuart asked.

"He's at the department store," their mother said.

"Then why do you want to go to the pet store?" Stuart asked.

"Santa isn't going to bring you a pet this Christmas," his mother said sadly. "We talked about that already."

"But, Ma," Lem said. "Marsha and Donald are getting pets for Christmas. Now I'm going to be the only Pet Lover without a pet."

"Pets cost money," his mother said.

"Even if Santa brings them?" Stuart asked.

"Even if Santa doesn't bring them, you can get them for free," Lem said. "People are trying to find homes for pets all the time."

His mother folded her arms against her chest. "It costs money to feed them and give them the shots they need," she said. "Santa doesn't pay for that."

Suddenly Stuart looked up in alarm. "Does Santa know we moved?" he asked.

"Yeah," Lem said. "Ma called him just before we left the old house."

"Santa has a phone?" Stuart asked, happy and excited again. "You mean I could call him?"

Lem saw his mom sending him her don't-you-dare-say-a-word look.

"No, honey," she said to Stuart. "Santa doesn't have a phone. He just knows what kids want for Christmas."

"Only kids don't always get everything they ask for, do they," Lem said.

He watched Stuart holding up his paper chain.

It had almost a dozen crooked links to it.

His mother poured the cranberries into a bowl and put it on the table too.

His mom threaded a needle. She put a popcorn on first. Then a cranberry. Then a popcorn.

"Can't I go to the pet store just to look?" Lem asked.

"I can't stop you," his mother said.

"But I can't go to the pet store unless you

take me," Lem explained. "They don't let kids under twelve in there unless a grown-up goes with them. Please, Mom!"

"You'll only start wanting a pet more than you do now," his mom said gently.

"It doesn't hurt to dream, does it?" Lem asked.

"Sometimes it hurts," his mother said. "If you want things you're not going to get."

Lem walked upstairs to his room.

Above his bed were the pictures he had cut from the magazines and newspapers. Taped in a circle were pictures of dogs, cats, birds, fish, even mice. At the center of the circle was a big empty space.

That space belonged to Lem's pet. Just as soon as he knew what kind of pet he was going to have, Lem was going to tape its picture there—and it didn't matter how much the pet cost either!

Chapter 4

It was the first day of Christmas vacation.

Lem and Wylie were slipping and sliding their way down Pulaski Street toward Dr. Miller's.

Dr. Miller was standing beside the van.

All the other Pet Lovers were already inside.

Lem and Wylie jumped in the front.

Dr. Miller made sure all the doors were shut. Then he got in too.

Last year he had retired from being a vet, but Dr. Miller didn't look old. As far as Lem was concerned, what Dr. Miller looked was very, very tall. Even when he bent down so a Pet Lover could whisper in his ear, Dr. Miller was tall.

Lem turned around in his seat.

Becka and Norris and Bernie were sitting in the seat just behind.

Dirty Donald, Erin, Tammy, and Marsha were sitting at the back.

"How come you're so quiet today?" Wylie asked.

"No reason," Lem said. "I'm just quiet."

He had been thinking about Christmas and pets again and it had made him sad. Sometimes talking about things made bad feelings go away. But Lem was afraid that telling Wylie how he was feeling would only make him feel worse.

"Everybody remember the rules when we're on a field trip?" Dr. Miller asked, starting the engine.

"No screaming at the top of your lungs!" Becka shouted.

Everybody laughed, Dr. Miller included, because Becka had shouted it at the top of her lungs.

"No hitting!" Bernie said.

"No biting!" Tammy added.

"No leaving the group on your own," Dirty Donald said.

"Even if you have to go to the bathroom something awful," Norris added.

Nobody laughed at that. The Pet Lovers knew how horrible that could be.

Dr. Miller turned the van onto Smathers Street.

Lem saw the Christmas displays in the store windows. He watched the shoppers going into the stores and he saw more shoppers, carrying big bundles, coming out of them.

The van turned onto Kennedy Boulevard.

That was where Turkey Hill Elementary was.

"No more teachers, no more books," Dirty Donald chanted.

"You can't sing that yet," Erin said firmly.

"How come?" Donald asked.

"Not until June when we get turned into fourth-graders," Bernie said.

"*If* we get to be fourth-graders," Marsha moaned.

Lem turned around.

Marsha was looking as worried as she sounded.

Even if her family was rich, Lem couldn't help feeling a little worried *for* her.

Dr. Miller stopped the van in front of an enormous stone building.

The front doors were massive, wooden planks twelve feet tall.

CITY ZOO read the sign over the front doors.

"It looks like a prison," Erin said sourly.

"A prison for animals," Norris added.

Dr. Miller turned off the ignition. He got out of the van and helped the Pet Lovers out.

"Our zoo is old," he said as he led the kids across the parking lot, "but the animals here are very well taken care of."

The front door was so heavy that Dr. Miller had to lean against it to open it.

The Pet Lovers followed Dr. Miller into the main hall.

Lem looked around at the cold, stone walls.

He looked up at the ceiling almost three stories above him.

At one side was the admissions gate.

Only a few people were lined up there.

Lem shuddered. This zoo did feel like a prison.

A woman was walking toward them. She was not much older than Lem's mom.

"Miss Mulavey," Dr. Miller said as he shook her hand. "I'd like you to meet the Pet Lovers."

"Hi, Pet Lovers," Miss Mulavey said with a great big smile on her face.

"Miss Mulavey is the director of the zoo," Dr. Miller explained.

"Director?" Lem asked. "You're really important!"

"She's a VIP!" Tammy exclaimed.

"What's that?" Dirty Donald asked.

"A Very Important Person," Tammy said.

Miss Mulavey smiled. "I'm really glad to take the Pet Lovers on a tour of the zoo," she said.

"Does that mean the Pet Lovers are VIPs too?" Lem asked.

"It certainly does," Miss Mulavey said. "We always need more animal lovers."

"Hooray! Hooray! Hooray!" shouted the Pet Lovers happily.

"How about taking a look at some VIAs now?" Miss Mulavey asked.

"VIAs?" Lem asked.

"Why, Very Important Animals, of course," Miss Mulavey said, laughing.

Lem smiled. If someone as nice as Miss Mulavey was head of the zoo, he guessed it wasn't a prison, after all.

"Which VIAs should we see first?" Miss Mulavey asked.

"The monkeys," Becka shouted.

"Shhhhh!" went the Pet Lovers.

"The monkeys," Becka whispered.

"I want to see the polar bears," Norris said eagerly.

"The lions," Tammy suggested, "I *love* cats."

"How about you, Wylie?" Dr. Miller asked.

"I want to see the penguins," Wylie said.

"Does the zoo have any parrots, Miss Mulavey?" Marsha asked.

"We have several," Miss Mulavey said.

"I'm getting one for Christmas," Marsha said. "Do you know how much it's going to cost?"

"*One thousand dollars!*" the rest of the Pet Lovers shouted all together.

Lem saw that he and Marsha were the only Pet Lovers who didn't laugh at that one.

Erin stepped forward. "Lem's the newest member of the Pet Lovers," she said. "Let's let him choose."

Lem put his index finger to his chin.

It was how he thought best.

"How about the reptiles?" he asked.

The Pet Lovers were nodding their heads excitedly.

"Oh, yes," Tammy squealed.

"The reptiles are the wildest!" Dirty Donald agreed.

"What are reptiles?" Norris asked. "Tell me, please."

"We'll *show* you," Miss Mulavey said as she started down the corridor.

Some of the Pet Lovers walked with Miss Mulavey.

The others walked behind with Dr. Miller.

Down one long corridor.

Up another.

Clack! Clack! Clack!

The footsteps on the linoleum echoed against the stone walls.

"How come there aren't any Christmas decorations at the zoo?" Tammy asked.

"Animals don't celebrate the holidays is why," Bernie said.

"That's terrible," Tammy said. "They don't know what they're missing."

Miss Mulavey patted Tammy on the shoulder.

"I agree," Miss Mulavey said. "We just don't have the money in our budget right now. But maybe someday we'll be able to do Christmas at the zoo!"

At the end of the hall was a sign saying REP-TILE HOUSE.

Beneath the sign were two swinging doors.

Dr. Miller pushed one.

Miss Mulavey pushed the other.

Lem followed the rest of the Pet Lovers into another large room.

"Why is it so warm?" Marsha asked.

"And it's so damp too!" Norris exclaimed.

"It's yucky!" Erin said.

Miss Mulavey laughed. "But not for reptiles. Human beings can make their own heat, but reptiles depend on the atmosphere around them to stay warm."

On three sides were great walls of glass.

Miss Mulavey led them to one side of the room.

The Pet Lovers looked through the glass.

There, just on the other side of the glass, was a miniature garden. A tropical-looking bush grew at one side. On the floor was grass. Lem looked closer. Something was slithering through the grass.

"Yeeek!" Norris squealed. "I didn't know reptiles meant snakes!"

"Let me out of here!" moaned Wylie.

The other Pet Lovers laughed.

"We should have gone to the polar bears," Norris sighed. "Reptiles are creepy!"

"That's why I like reptiles," Dirty Donald said, "because they're so scary-looking."

"There are many different kinds of reptiles," Miss Mulavey observed, "and almost all of them scare human beings a lot. But the fact is that most reptiles are very peaceful, unless someone bothers them."

"What *other* kinds of reptiles are you talking about?" Norris asked suspiciously.

"Don't worry," Tammy said. "What could be scarier than snakes?"

"Well, let me show you," Miss Mulavey said happily.

She led the kids across the room.

That side of the room had no glass wall. Instead it had a gate that went all the way up the ceiling.

Lem gasped as he stuck his head between the bars.

It looked as if an entire swamp had been built inside the zoo.

There were the trees and grasses. There were

caves in the rocky walls. In the middle of it all, down below, was an enormous pond.

"But I don't see any animals!" Wylie said. "There's nothing there to be afraid of, Miss Mulavey."

"Do you see those eyes sticking out of the water, kids?" Miss Mulavey asked. "If you look close, you can see the nostrils."

Lem stuck his nose against the gate. "I don't see anything at all," he said.

Miss Mulavey pointed to a bridge on the far side of the swamp.

A man with a bucket stood there, holding a bucket.

He reached into the bucket for some fish.

He threw them into the pond.

Suddenly, an enormous creature was swimming through the swamp.

The largest jaws Lem had ever seen shot into the air.

The animal was devouring the fish.

"It's an alligator!" Dirty Donald wailed.

"It's really a crocodile," Miss Mulavey said.

"How can you tell the difference?" Norris asked.

"An alligator has a broader, more rounded

snout," Miss Mulavey explained. "A croc's snout comes to more of a point. But they come from the same family."

"They're like brothers, you mean?" Tammy asked.

"More like cousins," Miss Mulavey said.

"It eats raw fish," Norris groaned. "Even Donald wouldn't eat raw fish!"

"If someone would give me a raw fish to eat," Donald said, shrugging, "I'd give it a try!"

"Oh, crocs can eat lots of things," Miss Mulavey said cheerfully when the Pet Lovers had finished groaning at Donald. "They can eat birds and turtles and even an occasional human being."

"No!" Erin exclaimed.

"How can crocs do that?" Lem asked. "Birds fly so high and humans don't go into swamps very often."

"Did you see the croc's tail?" Miss Mulavey asked.

Just then the croc flipped itself awkwardly out of the water.

It waddled on its short legs up the muddy bank.

"The tail." Bernie sighed. "It's so long!"

"And very strong too," Miss Mulavey said.

"When a bird is flying nearby, or when a human being is walking on the bank, the croc can use its tail to strike a blow. That knocks the prey off its feet or out of the air, and then the croc really goes to work."

"With that awful mouth," Norris groaned.

"And those terrible teeth!" Tammy moaned.

"Oooh!" the Pet Lovers moaned along with her.

"It looks so mean!" Marsha said. "Imagine it eating birds. It ought to be ashamed!"

"There wasn't any crocodile the last time we came to the zoo," Bernie said.

"Oh, we just got the croc a month or so ago," Miss Mulavey said.

Lem watched the crocodile lying in the mud.

It didn't look mean at all to him.

Lem wondered if the croc felt lonely.

He wondered if the croc felt different too.

"If I ever came face to face with it, I'd scream!" Bernie said.

"I'd run!" Norris said.

"How about you, Lem?" Dr. Miller asked gently. "What would you do?"

"Oh, I don't know," Lem said. "Maybe I'd give it a hug!"

Lem heard the other kids laughing but he didn't mind.

He knew what it was like to be new.

"Does it have a name, Miss Mulavey?" Lem asked.

"Not yet," Miss Mulavey said. "Do you have any suggestions, Lem?"

"What do you think about Crocky?" Lem asked eagerly.

"It sounds just right to me," Miss Mulavey said. "But it's what the crocodile thinks that matters most!"

"Hello, Crocky!" Becka yelled.

The crocodile didn't move.

"Hello, Crocky!" Wylie yelled.

This time the crocodile turned its head, away from the kids and toward the swamp grass near him.

"Well, maybe another time," Miss Mulavey said.

"Maybe you'll come up with another name too," Becka said.

"But his name should be Crocky," Lem insisted. "He just *is* Crocky. I *know* it!"

"You really like that crocodile, don't you, Lem?" Dr. Miller said.

Lem nodded. "He looks so neat," he said, excitedly.

"If you like it so much, why don't you adopt it?" Erin suggested.

"How do you do that?" Lem asked.

"Well, some zoos have an Adopt-a-Pet program," Erin said. "You come to visit your pet all the time and you get a certificate too."

"That sounds wonderful," Lem said eagerly.

"It *is* wonderful," Miss Mulavey said. "But we don't have that program here at our zoo."

"Because of no money?" Norris asked.

"Same old problem, I'm afraid," Miss Mulavey said as she led the kids toward the next doors. "Next we'll see the monkeys," she said.

"Hooray! Hooray! Hooray!" the other Pet Lovers shouted.

"The monkeys are the best part," Becka said firmly.

"No, the birds are the best," Marsha corrected.

"No," Norris said firmly. "The polar bears are the best part!"

Lem knew he was already looking at the best part.

"Bye, Crocky!" Lem yelled down to the crocodile.

Suddenly the crocodile turned its head toward Lem.

"Hi, Crocky!" Lem yelled louder.

As Lem waved at the crocodile, the crocodile looked him straight in the eye. When he waved harder, Lem was all but certain that the great big crocodile was giving him a great big crocodile grin!

Chapter 5

"*T*sssss!"

Lem opened his right eye.

"*Tssssss!*"

He opened his left eye.

All night he had been dreaming of swamps with muddy banks and the crocodile he now called Crocky. It had been so nice that Lem decided to ignore the hissing noise, wherever it was coming from, and dream some more.

Something crackled downstairs.

Then it hissed again.

He sniffed.

Something smelled good. Very, very good.

All at once it came to him.

"Grandpa!" Lem shouted as he jumped out of bed and ran to the top of the stairs. "Is that you making that noise, Grandpa?"

"It's my bacon, Lem," Grandpa Kelley yelled from downstairs. "Get it while it's hot."

Lem ran back into his room.

He threw on his clothes as fast as he could.

On the floor beside his bed were the library books.

Lem grabbed them all and ran downstairs to the kitchen.

As soon as Lem saw his grandfather, he ran into his arms.

Grandpa Kelley's hugs were the best.

So was the bacon he always brought from the farm. Lem tried not to feel sad that there wasn't going to be any more now that the farm was sold.

"I'm real glad you're here, Grandpa," Lem said.

"Me, too," his grandfather said.

He was a big man, not as tall as Dr. Miller, but bigger around. His cheeks were ruddy from working outside and he wore overalls and a flannel shirt. No matter where he went, he'd always look like a farmer.

"When did you get here, Grandpa?" Lem asked.

"Last night," Stuart said before Grandpa Kelley could say a word. "After we were in bed."

Lem put his books next to his cereal bowl. Then he sat down.

"Where's Mom, Grandpa?" he asked.

"She had a job interview to go on," Stuart said.

"You mind letting Grandpa speak?" Lem asked.

"I'm just trying to help," Stuart said.

"I didn't know Ma had an interview," Lem said.

"One of the agencies called half an hour ago," Grandpa said as he put a plate of steaming hot bacon on the table.

"You think she's going to get something?" Lem asked.

"She thinks it's looking good, Lem," his grandfather said.

"Our luck's changing, Grandpa," Lem said. "I knew it would happen. Just in time for Christmas too!"

Lem picked up *Crocs on Parade!* and *Go 'Gators!* and showed them to Grandpa Kelley.

Stuart pointed to the cover of *Marsh Madness*.

"Is that an alligator?" he asked. "Or is it a crocodile?"

"That's a crocodile," Lem said.

"Yuck!" Stuart groaned. "No lips."

Stuart held the cover next to his face. He sucked in his mouth so he didn't have any lips either.

"It's hard to tell the difference," Grandpa Kelley said.

"No, it isn't," Lem said. "Stuart has a bigger mouth than a croc."

Stuart pounded the table with his spoon.

"Hey, Grandpa!" he whined.

"Lem!" Grandfather Kelley cautioned.

"Oh, you mean the difference between a croc and an alligator," Lem said, trying not to giggle.

Before Lem could say what the difference was, he heard a rapping at the door.

Grandpa opened the door.

Wylie stomped the snow from his boots and stepped inside.

"You're Grandfather Kelley," Wylie said, holding out his hand. "You just sold your farm and that's your pickup outside."

"Who are you, son?" Grandpa Kelley asked.

"He's Wiley Price," Stuart said, "from next door."

"Don't mind Stuart," Lem said.

"Couldn't have said it better myself," Wiley admitted. "You want to go see the snow pets, Lem?"

"What are snow pets?" Grandpa Kelley asked.

"Other kids make snowmen when it snows," Lem explained. "The Pet Lovers make snow dogs and snow cats."

"Don't forget snow hamsters!" Wylie chimed in.

"I want to see snow pets!" Stuart announced. "Take me with you!"

"I'm going to the library too," Lem said.

"You went to the library yesterday," Stuart moaned. "Library's boring."

"They have eight more books on crocodiles there," Lem explained, "but I can't take them out until I return these."

"I'll take you to see the snow pets a little later, Stuart," Grandpa Kelley said.

"Thanks, Grandpa," Lem said, grabbing his coat from the hook by the door.

He sat down to strap up his boots.

"See you around," Lem said as he opened the door.

"Nice to meet you, Mr. Kelley," Wylie said.

The two boys walked along Blueberry Lane.

"Library first or snow pets first?" Wylie asked.

"Snow pets first," Lem said.

They turned at Pulaski Street.

They walked by Bernie's house.

Bernie was in the front yard, wrapping an old woolen muffler around his snow dog's neck.

Bernie's dog Elton was standing next to the snow dog.

"It looks just like Elton," Lem said.

"Elton's not white," Bernie said.

"In a couple of days, the snow won't be so white either," Wylie said cheerfully.

Next door, Erin was packing snow into a peculiar shape.

"What's that you have there?" Wylie asked.

"It's a rabbit ear!" Erin said proudly. "What else would I have but a snow rabbit?"

"It's nice," Lem said.

The boys walked on till they came to Marsha's house.

Lem looked up on the roof to see how Santa and his reindeer were doing.

By the front walk, Marsha was busy, making a snow bird.

"You like my parrot?" Marsha asked.

"It's okay," Wylie said cautiously.

"My real bird is going to be all sorts of wonderful, glorious colors," Marsha said excitedly. "Not just boring old white."

"Is it all those colors that make your parrot so expensive? Huh?" Wylie asked.

Lem looked at Wylie.

He was trying hard not to giggle.

But the harder they tried, the worse the giggling got.

"Hey, it's *mean* to giggle that way!" Marsha said.

"Aw, come on, Marsha." Wylie giggled again. "I'm just teasing."

"Well, it's just that my bird is very exotic," Marsha said.

"It's not the only exotic pet in the world!" Wylie said.

"Well, it's a lot more exotic than a hamster, Wylie," Marsha said.

"How *dare* you say hamsters aren't exotic," Wylie said.

"Well, I guess a hamster's better than nothing." Marsha sighed as she turned sadly to Lem.

"Huh?" Lem asked.

"I mean it's too bad that you're not getting a pet," she said. "That's all."

"He said he could get one as soon as he decided what kind," Wylie reminded her.

"But still it's tough being the only Pet Lover without a pet, isn't it?" Marsha asked. "It's nice to have some kind of pet, even if most people can't afford anything as exotic as a parrot!"

Lem felt his face getting red. He hated having Wylie come to his rescue. He glanced at the books he was carrying. He saw the photo of the crocodile on the cover of *Marsh Madness*.

He thought of Crocky back at the zoo.

"A crocodile is more exotic," Lem said.

"Crocodiles are disgusting!" Marsha said.

"They're beautiful," Lem insisted.

"Well, it doesn't matter," Marsha said, "because no kid ever got a crocodile for Christmas!"

Lem bit down on his lip again. Most of the time it had made him sad to feel poorer than the other kids. But now he was beginning to feel mad instead. For once, Lem was fed up with being poor!

"Well, *I'm* getting a crocodile for Christmas!" Lem announced.

"You are not!"

"This year too!" Lem boasted.

"Why, a person with a pet crocodile would need an indoor swamp," Marsha protested.

"Oh, we're working on that," Lem declared happily. "Down in the basement. We've got more than a dozen men digging it all up. I'm having a Crocodile Christmas. That's for sure."

Lem bit down on his lip, but not because he was nervous.

Now the hurt kept him from bursting into giggles.

He looked at Wylie.

Wylie was having an even harder time.

"How come I didn't hear about this earlier?" Marsha asked suspiciously.

"Well, I didn't want you to feel bad because you're just getting some dumb bird," Lem said sweetly.

"You promise you're telling the truth?" Marsha asked cautiously.

"I really, *really* promise I mean it," Lem said.

"Well." Marsha hesitated. "Maybe I was wrong about your crocodile."

"You were wrong about hamsters too," Wylie said.

"I was not," Marsha said defiantly. "Hamsters *are* ordinary!"

Lem couldn't say a word now. It was too hard to keep from giggling. But the harder he tried not to giggle, the worse the giggling became.

He grabbed Wylie's arm and pulled him down the street.

Both of them were giggling and gasping for air at the same time.

When they got to the corner, they stopped.

"Wow, that'll keep Marsha from feeling sorry for you," Wylie said.

Lem stopped laughing. "What are you talking about?" Lem asked.

"Well, that's how all the kids feel about your not getting a pet for Christmas," Wylie said.

Lem felt his stomach do a flop. "They feel sorry for me?" he asked.

"Well, a little," Wylie admitted. "But it's just

because we all like you so much and we all know your mom doesn't have any money."

Lem's shoulders sagged. His stomach did another flop. Anybody feeling sorry for you was bad. But when it was your best friend feeling that way, it was a million times worse.

"But you shouldn't feel sorry," Lem said. "It's true what I said."

"What's true?" Wylie asked.

"I *am* getting a crocodile for Christmas, Wylie," Lem insisted.

"Where'd your family get the money?" Wylie asked.

"My grandpa sold his farm," Lem said. "And my mom got a real important job. We have lots of money now."

"And you're really getting a crocodile for Christmas?"

"Believe me, Wylie," Lem assured him. "I'm going to have a Crocodile Christmas!"

"You're kidding!" Wylie said.

Lem started to run down the street.

"Last one to the library is a silly old parrot!" he shouted over his shoulder.

So what if he hadn't been telling the truth, Lem thought.

Anything had to be better than having people feel sorry for you!

And right now, as Lem realized how happy Wylie was for him, and how envious Marsha was, Lem felt better than he had in a long, long time!

Chapter 6

After the library, they had sandwiches and hot chocolate over at Wylie's.

After sandwiches, they went sledding in the park.

Lem lost one of his new crocodile books in the snow and it took the two of them almost an hour to find it.

When Lem got back to his house, it was already getting dark outside.

"I'm home!" he shouted.

He slammed the kitchen door behind him.

For once Stuart wasn't sitting at the kitchen table.

No one else was there either.

Lem kicked off his boots.

He wriggled out of his winter coat.

Clutching his library books, he ran into the living room.

"Ma!" he shouted. "I'm home!"

But no one was in the living room either.

Lem ran upstairs.

No one there either.

"Where's everybody?" he shouted.

No answer.

He ran into his room.

He turned on the light.

He dropped the library books on his desk.

On the top of the books was the *National Geographic* the librarian had said he could keep.

On the cover was a picture of a crocodile.

Lem tore off the cover and taped it to the blank space at the center of all the other animal pictures.

Perfect!

Crocodile Christmas!

It made Lem want to laugh out loud.

Christmas was only four days away.

Lem thought of Crocky all alone at the zoo this Christmas and suddenly Lem felt sad. He wished he really could have a crocodile for Christmas. He wished it could be Crocky too!

Swoosh!

Pwishhh!

Lem heard something outside.

He went to his window.

Three figures were coming from the woods behind the house.

They were dragging something.

They were coming toward the house!

Lem shivered as he hid behind the curtain.

After a moment, he peeked around the curtain.

In the light of the streetlamp, he saw three shadows.

Lem let out one long sigh of relief.

"Ma!" he yelled as he burst out of his room.

"Grandpa!" he yelled as he ran down the stairs.

"Stuart!" he yelled as he ran into the kitchen.

Grandpa Kelley were carrying one end of an evergreen tree through the doorway.

Stuart was at the other end. Most of him was hidden by the branches he was hoisting above his head.

Lem's mom followed, carrying an old saw.

"Where were you, guys?" Lem asked.

"Getting the Christmas tree," Grandpa Kelley said.

"Grandpa sawed it down," Stuart said.

Lem followed everyone into the living room. Stuart was pushing the old Christmas tree stand between the two front windows. Grandpa and Mom angled the trunk of the evergreen into it.

"Nice," his mother said. "Very nice."

"It's beautiful," Stuart said.

"You're darn right," Grandpa Kelley said in his booming voice.

Lem tried to like it but he couldn't. The tree reminded him they didn't have the money to buy a tree this year. All afternoon he'd been happy being rich in front of Marsha and Wylie. Now he remembered sadly it had all been just-pretend.

"The job," he said. "You didn't get it, did you?"

"We'll talk about it later," his mom said.

"You'd be out *buying* a tree if you'd got the job," Lem said.

His mother was smiling.

But it was the brave smile.

Stuart dragged two cartons from the closet.

One was full of Stuart's paper chains.

The other was full of the popcorn-and-cranberry chains his mother had made the night before.

"It's going to be a real old-fashioned Christmas," Grandpa Kelley said happily. "With old-fashioned, homemade decorations!"

"What happened to all our electric light bulbs, Ma?" Lem asked.

"Oh, they wore out, honey," his mother said.

"It costs too much to get new ones?"

"Well, not all that much," his mother admitted. "But these decorations are practically free."

Stuart took one of his paper chains from the cardboard carton.

Grandpa Kelley was lifting him into the air.

Stuart draped the paper chain around the top of the tree.

"Why don't you join in, Lem," his mother suggested.

"Oh, heck," Lem said, "I wasn't much help with the decorations and I didn't help get the tree."

"I don't think they'd mind," his mother said.

She went into the kitchen.

Lem shrugged and followed.

"Would you still like to go to the pet store?" his mother asked.

"You changed your mind?" Lem asked happily. "How come?"

"If you say you won't be disappointed about not getting a pet of your own, I should believe you," his mother explained.

She put the pot on the stove.

"Oh, I don't think I'll get my hopes up about anything at the pet store, Ma," Lem said, smiling. "The pet I want isn't there."

His mother turned to him. "You know what you want now?"

"I want a crocodile, Ma!" Lem said.

"Oh, Lem!" his mother said, shaking her head. "What am I going to do with you?"

"It's what I want, Ma," he said firmly.

"Well, you won't find a crocodile under your Christmas tree," his mother said. "You've got to be sensible, Lem."

"I didn't say I expected to get one," Lem explained. "I just said I wanted one."

"Now, Lem," his mother said. "I don't want to hear another word about crocodiles."

"Sure, Ma," Lem said as he shrugged and walked out of the room.

Not another word.

He could handle that.

But he could still dream.

Chapter 7

DONT

WALK

Lem and his mother waited at the corner.

The light was taking forever to change, the way it always did when it was cold and windy.

The silver stars and bells that hung over the street rattled in the wind.

The people on the sidewalks held on to their hats.

Lem saw Norris.

He and his mom were waiting on the other corner.

WALK

Finally!

Lem's mom held out her hand.

"I'm eight, Ma!" he said as he stuck his hands into his pockets.

Lem walked a step behind her.

"Hi, Norris," Lem said, stopping at the white line in the middle of the street.

"Croco-doodle-doo, Lem!" Norris chanted happily.

"You're a rooster today?"

"Not cock-a-doodle-doo," Norris said. "*Croco*-doodle-doo!"

"What did you say?" Lem asked.

But the light changed again before Norris could say anything.

"What was that about?" Lem's mother asked as she pulled Lem to the other side. "Does he want a crocodile too?"

"Beats me," Lem said.

Lem followed his mother through the mob of shoppers.

Past Price Whompers Supermarket with the Christmas candy and cookies and plastic evergreen trees in the window.

Past the Hobby Shop with the games in the window.

Past the clothes store with the dummies staring into space.

When they came to a window with a dozen cocker spaniel puppies, they stopped.

PET WORLD was written in an arc at the top of the window.

"How about a cocker spaniel, Lem?" his mother asked. "Next year, I mean."

"Don't think so," Lem sighed.

"We'd be able to afford one after I get a job," his mother said.

"Crocs are a lot tidier," Lem pointed out.

"But puppies are adorable," his mother said.

"Do *you* want a pet, Ma?" Lem asked.

His mom smiled, but she didn't say a word as they stepped inside.

To one side was the Kitty Korner.

Lem saw Tammy staring into one of the cages there.

Her mother was standing just behind her.

"You getting another cat?" he asked Tammy.

"Daphne wants a little brother or sister," she said. "Did they start your swamp yet?"

"Swamp?" Lem asked.

"The one that's going into your basement," Tammy said.

"Swamp, did you say?" Lem's mother asked.

"That's what Erin told me," Tammy said.

"Erin?" Lem's mother asked. "What's she got to do with it?"

"Oh, she heard it from Bernie," Tammy explained.

Lem bit his lower lip nervously.

It was beginning to make sense.

"I want to go now," he said anxiously.

He grabbed his mother's hand.

"What happened to your being eight?" his mother asked, laughing.

The store was getting crowded.

More kids. More parents. More grandparents.

More noise.

More coming. More going.

Lem pulled his mother along toward the back.

"What was Tammy talking about?" his mother asked.

"How would *I* know, Ma?" Lem said.

"But a swamp?" his mother asked.

"Look at the fish, Ma," Lem said nervously as he pointed to the row of aquariums set up against the wall.

"You like fish?"

"For dinner?" Lem asked.

"For a pet, I mean."

"I'd rather have them for dinner, Ma."

Against another wall were more tanks.

Except these tanks didn't have any water in them.

Lem looked closer.

"It's lizards!" Lem exclaimed.

"Oh, dear," his mother said, sighing.

"A gila monster!" Lem exclaimed. "I've seen that in books, Ma."

"It's scary-looking," his mother said.

Lem looked again. "It looks cute to me," he said.

"Oh, Lem," his mother sighed. "Reptiles are so frightening."

"But I like reptiles," Lem said. "Especially . . ."

Lem felt the tap on his back.

It was Dirty Donald.

He was eating half of a chocolate bar.

The other half was on his nose, his left cheek, and his chin.

Lem recognized Donald's older brother Phil beside him.

He was eating a chocolate bar too, only half of it wasn't on his face.

Maybe Donald wasn't going to be a slob the rest of his life, after all.

"Wow!" Dirty Donald said, only he was practically shouting. "What are *you* doing here?"

"Looking at pets," Lem said.

"Getting some smaller animals to feed to the one you're getting for Christmas?" Donald asked.

"Lem?" his mother asked. "Do you know what's going on here?"

"Well, not exactly," Lem stammered.

"A regular Crocodile Christmas," Dirty Donald went on. "Erin says the swamp is going in the basement, but Becka said your grandpa is going to build you a whole zoo!"

"What are you talking about, Donald?" Lem's mother interrupted.

"Nothing, Ma!" Lem pleaded.

"You call being a millionaire nothing?" Dirty Donald asked.

"Who's a millionaire?" Lem's mother asked.

"Oh, it's just some dumb little secret," Lem said.

"Oh, it's no secret," Dirty Donald said. "Marsha and Wylie told *everyone.*"

"*What* did they tell everyone?" Lem's mother asked.

"Everyone knows Lem's grandpa sold his farm for a million dollars and he's going to build Lem his own private zoo," Dirty Donald said. "And you got this terrific job and Lem is going to have his very own crocodile. Gee, some people have *all* the luck."

"You told the Pet Lovers that we're rich?" his mother asked.

"It's not what you think, Ma," Lem pleaded.

"Everyone felt so sorry because you were so poor," Dirty Donald said. "Now you're the richest kid in town!"

Lem's mother grabbed Lem's hand and started to pull him through the store.

"Come on, Ma!" Lem complained. "Everyone's looking."

"You've got some very serious explaining to do, Lem," his mother said as they reached the street.

Lem tried to pull his hand away once more.

It was no use. Her grip was too strong.

Lem tried to think it wasn't as bad as he thought.

But in his heart, he knew it was a whole lot worse!

Chapter 8

"To your room!"

"But, Mom!"

"How could you tell the kids we were rich?"

"Wylie and I were just kind of teasing Marsha," Lem tried to explain. "And then . . ."

The phone rang.

Another interview.

"We'll talk when I get back," his mom said. "But no Pet Lovers for you from now on, Lem!"

Lem felt his heart sink and his stomach do a flip. "No Pet Lovers?" he asked.

"Pet Lovers is nothing but trouble for you, Lem. It only makes you unhappy about not having things."

"But Ma," Lem cried angrily, "they're my friends."

"You don't lie to your friends," his mother said.

Then she hurried downtown.

"No Pet Lovers?" he asked again even though he was all alone now.

Every time he said it, he found himself getting madder and madder.

"No Pet Lovers?"

Lem raced up the stairs.

Bang!

He slammed the door shut.

He waited.

He opened the door.

Bang!

The house shook.

Lem waited for Grandpa to storm up the stairs.

Nothing.

He opened the door once again.

His grandfather's suitcase was in the hall.

Lem dragged it into his room.

He opened the drawers of his dresser.

Three pairs of socks.

A flannel shirt.

Eight pairs of underpants.

The new crocodile books from the library.

Lem dumped them into the suitcase.

There was a rap at the doorframe.

"What's going on?"

Stuart was standing in the doorway.

"You going somewhere?" Stuart asked.

"None of your business," Lem declared.

"Are you mad at me?" Stuart asked.

"I'm mad at Mom," Lem said.

Stuart shrugged and turned back into the hall.

Lem ran after him.

"I'm running away from home, but don't you dare tell," Lem said.

"Not even Grandpa?"

Lem relented. "Grandpa's okay to tell."

Lem untaped the photo of the crocodile from his wall and stuck it in the suitcase.

He closed the suitcase and dragged it to the kitchen.

Stuart ran down the stairs after him.

Grandpa Kelley was reading the newspaper.

"Lem's running away from home, Grandpa," Stuart said.

"Is that a fact?" Grandpa Kelley said, looking up from his paper.

Lem put on his boots and laced them up.

"You can't stop me, Grandpa!" he announced.

"Is that my suitcase you're taking with you?"

"It's okay, isn't it?"

"Take good care of it," his grandfather said. "I'll want it back eventually."

Lem pulled on his coat.

"I'm going," he said. "I mean it. I mean I *really* mean it."

"What do you want us to tell Mom?" Stuart asked.

"Just that I love her," Lem said. "And that it's all her fault."

Lem pulled on his mittens.

"You have any idea where you'll be staying?" Grandpa asked.

"Wylie's, probably," Lem said. "After Christmas, I'll probably go to Florida."

"Florida's nice in the winter," Grandpa Kelley said. "You don't want to miss Disney World."

"Good-bye, everyone," Lem announced. "Please, please don't anyone stop me! I really, really mean it!"

Lem grabbed for the doorknob, but his mittens were so thick that it was hard to get a grip.

"I *really* mean it," Lem said again as he fumbled with the knob. "Don't anyone *dare* stop me!"

"Help your brother with the door, will you, Stuart," Grandpa Kelley asked.

When Stuart opened the door, Lem dragged the suitcase outside.

He pulled it around the side of the house.

He got to the street and pulled the suitcase along the sidewalk.

Just as he got to Wiley's, he turned.

Grandpa and Stuart were standing a hundred yards away, watching him.

"You can't stop me!" Lem screamed. "Don't even try!"

"We're just watching," Grandpa Kelley called back.

"Oh," Lem said. "Don't even *think* you can stop me!"

Wylie was coming down the front steps of his house.

"Hey, what's going on?" Wylie asked.

"I'm running away from home," Lem said. "Can I stay with you?"

"How long?" Wylie asked.

"A month, maybe," Lem said uncertainly.

"I have to ask my mom first," Wylie said.

Lem sat on the suitcase, waiting till Wylie ran back.

"My mom says forget it," Wylie said.

"What's that?" Grandpa Kelley hollered.

"She said no!" Lem shouted back.

"We already have company for the holidays," Wylie explained.

"They already have company for the holidays!" Lem shouted to his grandfather.

"That's understandable!" Grandpa shouted back. "This time of year it happens a lot!"

It was getting colder now. Lem was starting to worry. "Where am I going to go now?" Lem asked.

"Maybe Wylie can help you find someplace else, Lem," his grandfather said.

"*Why* are you running away, Lem?" Wylie asked as he ran down the steps toward Lem.

"My mom says I can't be in Pet Lovers anymore," Lem explained.

Wylie gasped. "No Pet Lovers?"

Lem shook his head sadly. "Not for me," he said.

"What about your crocodile?" Wylie asked.

Lem thought about what Wylie would think if Lem told him there never was going to be a Crocodile Christmas. "She says I can't have a crocodile either," Lem said. "That's another reason I've *got* to run away from home."

"Come on," Wylie said. "I bet one of the other Pet Lovers will help you."

"You think so?" Lem asked.

"Pet Lovers pull together, Lem!"

Wylie took hold of one strap.

Lem took hold of the other.

Together they pulled the suitcase along Blueberry Lane.

When they came to Pulaski Street, Lem looked back.

His grandfather and Stuart were still following.

"I'm not coming home!" Lem called to them. "Don't beg!"

"We're just watching," Stuart said.

They passed Norris's house.

No one home.

"Bernie?" Lem shouted when they got to the Banks's house. "Can I come live with you?"

"No room," Bernie shouted back but in a moment he was walking along with Wylie and Lem.

Erin didn't have any room either.

But she wanted to help.

So did Tammy and Becka.

Once they knew why Lem was running away from home, they all wanted to help him.

The Pet Lovers marched along Pulaski Street.

Lem and Wylie in the lead, pulling Grandpa's suitcase.

Just behind them almost all the other members of the club.

And fifteen feet behind them, Grandpa and Stuart.

They came to Marsha's house.

Even though it was only just getting dark, the lights on the trees and bushes were already on.

Lem looked up at the roof.

The floodlight was already on the Santa and his sleigh.

The reindeer's legs were already moving.

"You want me to see if Marsha can put you up?" Erin asked.

Lem looked at the roof.

He looked at the ladder at the side of the house.

He looked down the street to where his grandfather and Stuart were standing.

"It's not *inside* the house where I want to be," he said at last. "Where I want to be is *on the roof.*"

"Mrs. Johnson wouldn't allow it!" Erin said.

"I can do it," Lem said, "if the Pet Lovers help."

"But what are you going to do up there?" Erin asked.

"What's it going to prove?" Wylie chimed in.

"I'm not going to run away," Lem said. "I'm going to protest. The way the big kids do!"

"But we'll get into trouble!" Becka whined. "All of us!"

"We'll all *fall* off before that!" Dirty Donald moaned.

"No way," Wylie said. "The roof is *flat.*"

"Oh, yeah," Donald admitted. "I guess all those reindeer got in my line of vision."

"Your not wanting to stand out in the cold is what got in your line of vision," Norris said, laughing.

"Okay," Donald said. "Count me in!"

"All for one and one for all," Lem reminded them. "Are you going to help me?"

"I'm in!" Wylie said.

"Me too!" Erin said.

"Me too!" shouted everyone else.

"Hooray! Hooray! Hooray!"

Before anyone could stop him, Lem headed for the ladder at the side of the house.

Chapter 9

There was snow on each rung of the ladder.

Lem wiped the snow off with one hand and clutched Grandpa's suitcase with the other.

Then, with his arms wrapped around the sides, he started climbing. By the time he reached the top, he was breathing hard.

The roof was flat. There was snow on it, but there was a wall all around the edge. You could slip and slide there, but once you got there, there wasn't any danger of falling off.

Wylie climbed up next.

Then Erin.

Then Becka and Norris.

Then Bernie and Tammy and Dirty Donald.

Just as Marsha got to the top, Lem saw Marsha's mom and dad running around the side of the house.

"Pull it up!" Lem shouted. "Quick!"

Lem took one side of the ladder.

Erin took the other.

The other Pet Lovers grabbed rung after rung.

It was only seconds before the Pet Lovers had the ladder resting on Marsha's roof.

"You kids come down!" Marsha's father shouted.

"Not until Lem's mother says he can stay in Pet Lovers," Marsha called back.

"It's not our business what Lem's mother does," her mother called up.

"We're Pet Lovers, Mrs. Johnson," Bernie shouted.

"Pet Lovers stick together!" Norris yelled.

Lem looked over the side of the roof.

People were gathering on the sidewalk. More were standing in the Johnsons' front yard.

At the front of the crowd stood Grandpa Kelley and Stuart.

"Hi, Grandpa," Lem yelled.

"We sure miss you, Lem!" Grandpa called up.

"You coming home for Christmas, Lem?" Stuart asked.

"Only if Lem can stay in Pet Lovers," Erin said firmly.

"Only if your mother gives Lem a crocodile for Christmas, too!" Dirty Donald called down.

The Pet Lovers gathered in a huddle by the edge of the roof.

"Crocodile Christmas!" the Pet Lovers chanted again and again. "Crocodile Christmas!"

The sun had set, but the roof was ablaze from the Christmas decorations.

The streetlamps were lit.

Drivers turned on their headlights.

More and more passersby were gathering in front.

More and more cars were driving past the house.

"I want to ride Donner!" Erin cried.

"I get Blitzen," Norris yelled.

"I want to sit in the sleigh next to Santa Claus," Tammy said.

"You guys be careful," Lem shouted. "Watch out for the electric cords!"

"Watch out for *anything* electric," Erin yelled.

In a flash, the Pet Lovers were running in all directions all over the roof.

Some of the kids were jumping on the reindeer.

Some of them were sitting next to Santa in his sleigh.

Car after car slowed as the passengers took a look at the fabulous Christmas display at the Johnsons' house.

Only now the Pet Lovers were the stars of the display!

Pulaski Street was turning into a major traffic jam!

Toot! Toot!

Honk! Honk!

In the distance, Lem heard a siren.

Soon a police car was winding its way through the traffic jam.

It pulled up at the Johnsons' house and a policeman with a moustache got out.

"Get another ladder!" the folks on the lawn were shouting.

"Get those kids down here!" someone yelled.

Lem saw his mother now.

She was darting through the crowd.

Lem saw the look on her face.

She was mad.

"Lem Ferris!" she shouted. "You come down here this instant!"

"Not till you let me stay in Pet Lovers!" Lem said.

"What's Pet Lovers?" the policeman interrupted.

"It's a club," Lem's mother explained.

"A club she wants me to quit!" Lem shouted.

"This is all because you won't let your son belong to some kids' club?" the policeman asked.

"She won't let him have a crocodile either!" Erin yelled down.

The policeman started to smile now.

"Gee, this sounds serious," he said, grinning. "How come you won't let your poor little boy have a crocodile?"

"Crocodile Christmas!" the Pet Lovers chanted again. "Crocodile Christmas!"

Soon the crowd was laughing too and chanting, "Crocodile Christmas! Crocodile Christmas!" along with the Pet Lovers.

"We're not leaving this roof until Lem gets his crocodile!" Bernie shouted.

"Is there any chance that Lem will have his crocodile in the near future?" the policeman asked Lem's mother.

Lem's mother shook her head firmly.

The policeman started to chuckle.

Then he started to laugh.

Soon most of the grown-ups were laughing too.

Except Lem's mother and Mr. and Mrs. Johnson.

"If those kids don't come down right away, this could turn into a regular riot," Mr. Johnson said.

"Right in our front yard!" Mrs. Johnson moaned.

Lem saw two other men making their way through the mob.

"Firemen!" Norris yelled.

Lem looked again.

He had no trouble identifying what they were carrying.

"A ladder!" Bernie groaned.

"I knew it!" Marsha wailed.

"Just like grown-ups to pull a stunt like that!"
Norris complained.

Lem watched the policeman leaning the ladder against the house. A moment later, he was climbing up toward the Pet Lovers.

His mom was climbing after them.

Then came the Johnsons.

Now there were more grown-ups on the roof than Pet Lovers.

Everyone was slipping and sliding all over the roof.

Lem tried to duck behind the chimney, but it was too late.

His mother had already spotted him.

Never had she looked so mad!

Lem grabbed his grandfather's suitcase and ran for the ladder.

One hand around the side of the ladder, the other hand holding the suitcase, he lowered himself rung by rung to the ground.

"Can I help you with that?"

Lem stepped back.

"Grandpa!"

"I'll take the suitcase for you, Lem," Grandpa Kelley said, reaching out for the bag.

"Okay." Lem sighed.

"You through running away from home?" Stuart asked, still holding on to Grandpa's other hand.

"For today, I guess," Lem said.

Then the three of them started walking their way through the crowd, toward home.

Chapter 10

Still no Mom.

It had been almost an hour since Stuart and Lem and Grandpa had come home. Every time Lem looked at the clock above the fireplace in the living room, he got more and more worried.

T R A
B A T
R A T

Stuart sat on the floor, playing with the blocks with the letters on them. "You're really going to get it this time," he said.

Lem leaned down and put the *B* block in front of the *R A T* blocks.

"*B R A T?*" Stuart asked.

"That's what you are," Lem said.

Stuart took the *I* and the *G* from the box.

B I G

"What's that supposed to mean?" Lem asked.

"How do you spell trouble?" Stuart asked.

"Big trouble?" Lem asked.

Stuart nodded. "That's what you're going to be in," he said sadly.

"*Very* big trouble," Lem agreed.

"How long will Mom make Lem stay in his room this time, Grandpa?" Stuart asked.

Grandpa Kelley sat by the fire. "About a million years," he said cheerfully.

"But, Grandpa," Lem said, "even bank robbers don't get a million years!"

"That's because your mother isn't the judge," Grandpa said.

Lem heard the kitchen door slam.

"Ma?" he called. "Is that you?"

Silence.

"Ma?"

Still no answer.

"It's her," Lem said quietly.

"I'll protect you," Stuart said, scrambling to his feet.

Lem almost smiled. "Thanks, Stu," he said. "But I got to do it myself."

He walked down the hall to the kitchen.

His mother was hanging her coat on the hook beside the door.

"How come it took you so long, Mom?"

His mother shrugged. "That policeman wanted to talk to me," she said.

"About me?" Lem asked fearfully.

His mom didn't say a word.

Lem sighed. "You mad?" he asked in his softest voice.

His mom turned. "What do you think, Lem?" she asked.

Lem looked his mother in the eye. She didn't look like she was mad, but she didn't sound happy either. It drove him crazy when he couldn't figure her out.

"Well, you could be very, very, very mad," Lem said. "Or you could be just a tiny, little bit upset," he added hopefully, sitting down on the other side of the table. He put his hands behind his head and looked up at the ceiling.

"Oh?" his mother asked. "Me get upset just because you ran away from home?"

"Well, there's other things," Lem admitted.

"Really?" his mom asked. "Tell me about them."

"Well, you could be upset that I got the Pet Lovers involved," Lem said.

"But what are friends for if they won't go to bat for you?" his mother asked.

"That's an excellent point," Lem admitted. "But I should have handled it more on my own."

"How about the riot?" his mother asked.

"Everyone had a pretty good time, don't you think?" Lem said.

He laughed a little. But he stopped as soon as he realized his mom wasn't even going to crack a smile over it.

"You didn't have a very good time, huh?" he asked.

"Just because I won't let you have a crocodile for Christmas, it doesn't mean I don't have feelings, Lem," his mother pointed out. "It felt a little funny with all those thousands of people laughing at me."

"It wasn't more than a couple hundred, Mom," Lem reminded her. "And you can't take these things personally, Ma. It'll only get you depressed."

"Really?" his mother asked. "I have no idea what I'm even complaining about."

"Well, it's hard having *anyone* laugh at you sometimes," Lem said. Right now, he was feeling so sorry for her that he forgot about feeling sorry for himself.

"That's nice of you to say," his mother said.

"And it's especially hard when you've tried your best at something," Lem added.

Lem got out of his chair and walked around to her side of the table.

"Me?" his mother asked. "Try my best at *what*?"

"At being a mom," Lem said, putting his arm around her shoulder.

"You think so?"

"I think so and Stuart does too, Mom," Lem said. "Sometimes a parent just has to take a firm hand. You just got to show kids who's the boss."

"You really think so?" his mother asked.

"I mean, if a kid of mine went around shooting off his mouth . . ."

"The way you did at Pet Lovers?"

"Exactly," Lem said, "and telling everyone he was going to have a crocodile when he wasn't, and telling them his family had loads of money when they didn't, why I'd make him tell the truth."

"Even at Christmas?"

"You got to teach kids good habits or it'll be really tough on them when they grow up."

"Does that mean you're going to tell the Pet Lovers the truth, Lem?"

Lem felt a shiver going up his spine. "Huh?"

"You lied to them, Lem," his mother said.

"But, Ma!" Lem exclaimed. "Do you know what the Pet Lovers would think if I told them I'd lied?"

"Who cares what the world thinks?" his mother said. "Isn't that what you just told me?"

"But they'd kick me out! Couldn't I go to my room for the rest of my life instead?"

"Tell them the truth, son."

Lem turned around.

Grandpa Kelley was standing in the doorway.

"It's what you know you should do," Grandpa Kelley said.

"I was tricked into it," Lem exclaimed.

"You tricked yourself, Lem," his grandfather said.

Lem felt his shoulders sag.

He knew when he was outnumbered.

This time he knew when he was just plain wrong, too.

"It wasn't all a lie," he said. "I did want a Crocodile Christmas. Even if it's nuts, it's what I wanted."

"Maybe the Pet Lovers will understand," his grandfather said.

"But maybe they won't," said Lem.

"But you'll tell them?" his mother asked.

Lem nodded sadly. "Tomorrow's the weekly meeting," he said. "I'll tell them then."

"You need to apologize to your mom too," his grandfather said.

"Mom," he said, "I'm sorry about what happened to you at the riot. I'm sorry the policeman made you stay afterward too, Mom."

"He didn't make me stay," his mother said. "When he heard I was looking for a job, he asked me down to the station house. There's an opening there."

Lem looked up hopefully. "You got the job, Mom?"

His mother shook her head. "Don't get your hopes up." She sighed.

"Right," Lem said. "No use hoping for something you might not get. You might get hurt."

Then he left the room to go upstairs.

Chapter 11

Wylie stomped his boots on the front porch.

"You coming?" Wylie asked.

"Later," Lem said, opening the door a crack.

"I'll wait," Wylie said, "so we can walk together."

"You go ahead," Lem said. "I'll catch up."

He closed the front door.

Through the side window, Lem watched Wylie walking down Blueberry Lane.

He put on his coat, strapped up his boots, and found his mittens on the floor of the closet.

He went outside.

Stuart and Grandpa Kelley were cleaning out the back of the pickup.

"What you doing that for?" Lem asked.

"For fifty cents," Stuart said as he stuffed scraps of wood into a big black plastic bag.

"You don't want to walk with Wylie?" Grandpa Kelley asked.

"Not if he has to vote me out of the club," Lem said. "Wouldn't be fair."

His grandfather put his arm around Lem's shoulder.

"See you later," Grandpa Kelley said.

"If I live," Lem groaned.

Lem started down Blueberry Lane.

The sun was out and it was warmer than it had been in weeks.

The snow was melting.

The icicles were drip-drip-dripping from the roofs.

Water was whooshing through the gutters.

Lem walked on.

Around the corner and onto Pulaski Street.

Past Dr. Miller's house.

Past Norris's house.

When he passed Marsha's house, he didn't look up.

He didn't want it to hurt more than it did already.

When he got to Erin's house, he turned in at the gate.

From the basement, he could hear the Pet Lovers singing.

> "Pet Lovers are a noble breed.
> We're loyal, brave, and true.
> If you agree, come on and be
> A Pet Lover too!"

Slowly, Lem walked down the steps.

Just as he leaned against the door, he heard the Pet Lovers going "Hooray! Hooray! Hooray!" the way they always did at the end of the Pet Lovers anthem.

C–R–E–A–K.

"Lem?"

"Yeah?"

It took a second or two for Lem's eyes to focus.

"We were worried about you."

Lem blinked. Now he could see it was Erin leaning forward in her chair, talking to him.

"Wylie thought you might be sick or something," Bernie said.

"Just late," Lem said, taking the seat next to Norris. "Did any of you get in trouble for yesterday?"

"Well, I got a talking-to," Marsha admitted. "About going on the roof."

"Me too!" Norris said.

"My dad thought it was funny," Erin said, "as long as nothing like that ever happens again."

"My mom said it was understandable us wanting to help you out," Bernie said.

Lem smiled a little from relief.

It didn't make things good.

It made them just a little less bad.

"It was our duty as Pet Lovers to protest!" Becka said.

She jumped onto her feet and started waving her hands madly around in the air.

When the other Pet Lovers started laughing, her face got red and she sat down abruptly.

"Did you get in trouble, Lem?" Norris asked.

Slowly Lem nodded.

"Is your mom going to dock your allowance?" Bernie asked.

"Is she going to make you stay in your room?" Marsha asked.

Lem shook his head. "She says I have to tell the truth," he said.

"The truth?" Marsha asked.

"What truth?" Bernie asked.

"Tell *who* the truth?" Dirty Donald chimed in.

Lem sat forward in his chair. He thought of the Pet Lovers anthem. "Loyal, brave, and true," the anthem went.

Lem took a breath.

Exhale.

Not ready yet.

Deeper breath.

"My mom never even said I could have a crocodile for Christmas," he said. "I just said it. Because all along my mom said I couldn't have a pet this year and I didn't want anyone feeling sorry for me."

Lem looked down at his lap. He couldn't look at the Pet Lovers now. He couldn't bear to see how disappointed they must be. Maybe even hurt. Probably angry too.

Toot! Toot!

It came from the street.

"It was a mistake, that's all," Wylie said.

"The reason I can't have a pet is we don't have the money," Lem admitted. "I lied. I feel horrible about it."

Toot! Toot!

There it was again!

"You'll have a Crocodile Christmas *another* year," Wylie said as he patted Lem on the shoulder.

"But I *lied*," Lem said firmly. "I'm not loyal, brave, or true. I don't deserve to be a Pet Lover! You should probably take a vote right now."

"You want us to kick you out?" Erin asked.

"Oh, I wouldn't hold it against you," Lem assured them all. "You've got to make sure Pet Lovers stay loyal, brave, and true, don't you?"

"But you're our friend!" Tammy said.

"We like you too much!" Norris said.

"If you guys don't kick me out, I'm going to quit!" Lem declared as he jumped to his feet.

Toot! Toot!

Now there was pounding on the basement door.

"Hey, guys, let me in!" a little voice yelled. "Let me in!"

C–R–E–A–K!

The cellar door swung open.

Light filled the basement.

There in the doorway was Stuart.

"Out of here, everyone!" he yelled. "Follow me!"

The Pet Lovers were on their feet, grabbing their coats. Then they grabbed their pets.

They ran past Stuart, up the steps, around the side of the house, and down to the street.

Grandpa's pickup was at the curb.

The Christmas tree that had been in Lem's living room was now in the back, cranberry and popcorn, paper chains and all!

Across the side were letters, MERRY CHRISTMAS!

Grandpa Kelley was at the wheel. "All aboard, Pet Lovers!" he yelled.

"Where are we going, Grandpa?" Lem asked. "What's the Christmas tree doing on the truck?"

"Don't you mind," Grandpa Kelley said. "It's a surprise for the Pet Lovers!"

"But I'm not a Pet Lover anymore," Lem said sadly.

"Sure you are," Erin said.

"We haven't voted you out," Wylie reminded him.

"Not yet," Lem said. "But that's because you haven't had time!"

"I want you in Pet Lovers even if you're not getting a Crocodile Christmas," Wylie said.

"That's what I say!" Erin added.

"Me too!" Bernie shouted.

"But I lied!" Lem pleaded as he felt his eyes getting wet with the beginnings of little tears. "Isn't anyone listening to me?"

"Aren't you the boy who has been dreaming of a Crocodile Christmas?" his grandfather asked.

Lem nodded, but it was hard fighting back the tears now. "But it's not going to happen," Lem said. "No matter how hard I dream."

"Well, maybe you just gave up on your dream a little too soon," Grandpa Kelley said.

"Too soon?" Lem asked. "What's that supposed to mean?"

"Is Lem going to have a Crocodile Christmas, after all?" Tammy asked excitedly.

"Climb in back, Pet Lovers!" Grandpa Kelley exclaimed. "There's going to be a Crocodile Christmas for *everyone!*"

Chapter 12

"**A**ll aboard!" Grandpa Kelley yelled from the cab of the pickup to the kids standing in the back.

"All aboard!" shouted Stuart.

"All aboard!" shouted the Pet Lovers.

Grandpa put the motor into gear and the pickup pulled away from the curb.

Lem grabbed the side of the truck with one hand.

With the other, he held on to Stuart.

"Wheeeeee!" the Pet Lovers cried as the pickup picked up speed.

"Where's Grandpa Kelley taking us?" Wylie yelled.

"Crocodile Christmas was all he said!" Marsha exclaimed.

As Lem looked from face to face, he knew the Pet Lovers were every bit as excited as he was.

The pickup turned onto Smathers Street.

They passed Price Whompers and the pet shop.

"I bet *he* knows where we're going!" Erin said, pointing at Stuart.

Stuart smiled his Perfect Little Angel smile. "But I'm not telling!" he squealed.

"Come on! Tell!" the other kids yelled at him.

But Stuart shook his head harder and harder.

The Pet Lovers held on tight to their pets as the pickup turned another corner.

Past Turkey Hill Elementary.

Past the mall.

The faster the pickup went, the chillier and windier it got.

But the Pet Lovers were too excited to mind!

"Wheeeeeee!"

Another corner.

Another street.

They were slowing down in front of a big stone building.

"The zoo!" the Pet Lovers cried.

Grandpa Kelley stopped the truck and started to help the Pet Lovers out of the back.

He grabbed hold of the Christmas tree.

"The tree?" Lem asked. "You're taking it into the zoo?"

"It's Christmas, isn't it?" Grandpa Kelley asked.

"But, Grandpa," Lem said, "they won't let us in with a tree!"

But Grandpa Kelley wasn't listening.

Holding the tree with both hands, he led the Pet Lovers and their pets to the entrance.

Just as they reached the entrance, the doors opened.

There stood Miss Mulavey and Dr. Miller.

"Welcome, Pet Lovers," Miss Mulavey called.

"Merry Christmas, everyone!" Dr. Miller said.

"You knew we were coming?" Lem asked.

"Your grandfather called me this morning," Dr. Miller said.

"Then Dr. Miller called me," Miss Mulavey said. "We thought it was a great idea having Christmas at the zoo."

Miss Mulavey and Dr. Miller helped Grandpa carry the tree down the hall.

The Pet Lovers ran after them.

Down the hall.

Clack! Clack! Clack!

Lem saw the big swinging doors that led to the reptile house.

He saw the grown-ups go through.

There, in the middle of the room, was a table that hadn't been there before.

It had Christmas cookies and cakes on it and soft drinks too.

Behind the table was a lady Lem hadn't seen since breakfast.

"Hi, honey," the lady said.

"Mom!" Lem exclaimed. "What are you . . . ?"

"Your mom's half the brains behind all this," Grandpa Kelley explained.

"I got the job at the police station," his mother said.

"It's definite?" Lem asked.

His mother nodded happily. "You can have a pet at home now," she said. "But not a crocodile. Anything but a crocodile, Lem."

"*Anything,* Ma?" Lem teased.

"Okay," his mother said, laughing as she sighed. *"Almost* anything!"

Lem saw the kids racing around the room, waving at the snakes and gila monsters behind the glass.

"Can we sing carols?" Tammy asked Miss Mulavey.

"That's what we're going to do next," Miss Mulavey said.

"But not just to the reptiles, I hope," Marsha said.

"We'll sing carols to *all* the animals!" Dr. Miller said.

"What a terrific Christmas!" Marsha exclaimed.

"Wow!" Erin said.

"What a party!" Dirty Donald said as he stuffed two of the cookies into his mouth at the same time.

Lem ran to one side of the room.

He looked into the swamp.

"Crocky!" Lem yelled. "There's Crocky!"

As Lem waved and waved at Crocky, all the Pet Lovers ran up beside him and waved too.

"Well, it wouldn't be a Crocodile Christmas without him, would it?" Grandpa Kelley said.

"It wouldn't be Pet Lovers without Lem!" Wylie said.

"I make a motion that Lem Ferris is now and forever a member in good standing in Pet Lovers!" Erin yelled. "Do I hear a second?"

"Second!" all the Pet Lovers shouted.

"Hip! Hip! Hooray!" everybody, Miss Mulavey and Dr. Miller and Grandpa Kelley and Lem and Stuart's mom included, shouted.

Lem's smile went from ear to ear.

Miss Mulavey stepped forward, holding out a rolled up piece of paper with a red ribbon tied around it. "Read it, Lem," she said. "It's for you."

Eagerly Lem untied the ribbon and unrolled the scroll.

The words were in very official-looking handwriting.

THIS IS TO CERTIFY THAT
Mr. Lem Ferris
HAS FORMALLY ADOPTED
Crocky the Crocodile
IN THE CITY ZOO's *new* ADOPT-A-PET PROGRAM
AND QUALIFIES FOR ALL THE RIGHTS AND
RESPONSIBILITIES THAT COME WITH SUCH OFFICE.

At the bottom was a photograph of Crocky.

"Oh, thank you!" Lem said happily. "He's mine, isn't he?"

"Except Crocky stays here," Mrs. Ferris said nervously. "He can't bring him home, can he?"

"No," Miss Mulavey laughed. "Crocky stays here."

"You got the Adopt-a-Pet program?" Erin said excitedly. "When?"

"We just got the financing a few days ago," Miss Mulavey replied. "Sort of a Christmas present to the zoo. Lem and Crocky are our first official members."

She led Lem and all the others to the gate.

Dr. Miller and one of the zoo custodians were standing on the little bridge above the swamp now. They were setting the Christmas tree on the bank. Just then Crocky slipped out of the water and waddled across the mud. He looked up at the tree a moment, then waddled under it and lay down.

Lem felt his mom's hand on one shoulder.

"I guess I was wrong," his mother said happily. "There really is a crocodile under your Christmas tree!"

He felt his Grandpa's hand on the other.

"Thanks, Mom," he said. "Thanks, Grandpa."

"Merry Christmas, everybody!" Lem shouted.

"Merry *Crocodile* Christmas," shouted all the Pet Lovers, all together now.

Crocs and Gators

Crocodiles and alligators come from the same family of animals called crocodilians.

Of the crocodiles, the best known in the United States is the *Crocodylus acutus*. Their maximum size is fourteen feet, and they are found in the southernmost parts of Florida. In their native habitat, they show very little hostility toward human beings. In captivity, however, they can be very, very mean.

The *Alligator mississippiensis,* on the other hand, can be almost playful. Human beings can even walk on their backs as they lie in their marshes and they will not exhibit any angry behavior. Alligators also make their home in Florida, in the Everglades, but as human beings have swallowed up their natural habitat and their food sources, their length has gone from twenty feet long to less than twelve.

Sometimes one can find very small alligators —less than a foot in length—for sale as pets. In captivity, however, they often refuse to eat and consequently die from starvation.

Pet Lovers make pets only of animals who are happy in captivity and enjoy living in human homes. They leave the others—like crocodiles and alligators—in their native habitat!

The Pet Lovers Club Anthem

(To the tune of "Row, Row, Row Your Boat")

Don't forget to feed your pet
And check its water too!
When it's sick, go see the vet.
Your pet depends on you!

Clean its home out once a week,
Its hutch or cage or bowl.
Tend its broken tail or beak.
Pet Loving is our goal!

Pet Lovers are a noble breed.
We're loyal, brave, and true!
If you agree, come on and be
A Pet Lover too!